Black Widow;

A Collection of Science-Fiction & Horror Shorts ©2007

Edition1

written by:

Brandea DeBusk McGill

Black Widow; A Collection Of
Science-Fiction & Horror Shorts

by: Brandea DeBusk McGill

ISBN-978-0-6151-5834-1

Black Widow; A Collection Of
Science-Fiction & Horror Shorts

by: Brandea DeBusk McGill

ISBN-978-0-6151-5834-1

Table of Contents

Black Widow ©2007

He sat patiently, peering through the bush, waiting for the lights inside the house to go out. He knew he would not be seen, there was no moon shining tonight, and dark storm clouds hovered ominously overhead, threatening to unleash their heavy loads. He had broken the porch light earlier that day while the house was empty, and jimmied the lock on the sliding glass doors off the back deck. He could see her drying her hair through the upstairs bathroom window, and knew in only a matter of minutes she would be snug in her bed.

Lights out. Show time.

He grabbed his bag and headed for the deck, reaching it just before the rain began falling in heavy waves, crashing loudly against the roof and decking. *Perfect.* He could not have picked a better night. He pulled on the taut latex gloves, slid the door open, and carefully slipped inside. With carefully placed footsteps, he made his way up the stairs, cautiously avoiding the squeaky boards, toward her room. She was laying on her stomach, facing the window opposite the door. Rope in hand, he jumps on her, shoving her face hard into the pillow and placing his knee in the back of her head to hold her there. She struggled against him, but he managed to tie both her wrists behind her back. He turned her over to face him.

A scream.

Quickly securing her wrists to the bedpost, he then placed duct tape over her mouth.

" Shut up Bitch!!" He growled at her, slapping her for good measure. He grabbed more rope from his bag, tossed it onto the bed, and held his knife between his teeth as he tied each one of her legs to the bedposts. He straddled her, and held the knife to her throat,

"Now, we are gonna have us some fun." he said noticing the tears running down her cheeks, and the fear in her wide-eyed stare, she was trembling. He smiled, and tore her nightgown from her body, leaving her bare flesh exposed to his ravenous gaze.

Whimpering, tears.

"Now, now. We'll have none of that." he leaned in and whispered in her ear, flicking the fleshy lobe with his tongue. He slipped his hand into her panties, and sliced them from her body with his knife,then tossing them both to the side. He pulled off one latex glove with his teeth, and slung it to the floor. Reaching into his bag, he pulls out five fingernails he had fashioned himself from razor blades, and showed them to her one by one as he placed them on his fingers. He traces the curve of her face with one razor nail, and slowly digging into her skin. Small droplets of blood mix with tears that stain her face. Then, violently he slashes across her breast, shredding the delicate flesh, exposing bone.

She bucked and writhed with the pain. Then he was on top of her, inside her, she felt the razor nails running up the inside of her thighs as he moved within her. Then......

there was nothing, nothing but sweet blackness.

Weak bitch passed out. He thought as he zipped his pants, and began loading his bag. He heard something. The rain? Thunder? No! Someone was coming up the stairs! He turned to face the door..........gunfire!........he felt himself falter, falling.......

Trinity was devastated. One minute everything was perfect, and the next, her world came crashing down on her. Her entire life was based on lies and deceit. Everything she thought she knew no longer made any sense to her. Since the death of her husband she's been walking around in a blur, unaware, existing, *barely*. Now that the funeral was over, the police have been knocking on her door hounding her for information. He was shot to death, inside the home of a rape victim. By the husband who just happened to be a fellow police officer. They said he usually worked the night shift, but had gotten off early that night, and happened upon an intruder. *Micheal.* They think *her* husband was responsible for raping and torturing countless women in the area, all of them had husbands on the force. They had seemed just as shocked by the revelation themselves. Many of the guys had been to their house for dinner and barbecues. She had swapped recipes and lunch dates with many of their wives. It was all too much for Trinity. Too shocking.

" But, maybe he was there investigating the incident himself." She had told them, trying to process the whole thing. When they came to tell her the news she thought he had been killed in the line of duty. She could not believe it. Her husband, a police officer, and a *rapist*? It just did not make any sense. Micheal had been leading a double life.

She could be thankful for only one thing, she did not know the officer involved or his wife. She would not have to look into their faces. She didn't think she would ever be able to show her face in public again. After weeks of harassment, she finally convinced the police she knew nothing, *ever*. How could they even think she would know about something like that? In the six years they were married, she never had an inkling. Micheal had always been so gentle and loving to her. Finally the investigation was dropped, and the case closed. After all, Micheal was dead, and there was nothing else they could do. *It was done.* Trinity's best friend had moved in with her after Micheal's funeral. Sarah. Thank God for Sarah. She had been running all the errands and doing the shopping for the last six months. Trinity could not bear to go out in public. Not yet. She had become very secluded, shut herself off from the world. She never went outside the house anymore. The only interaction she ever had was with Sarah, her boyfriend Kevin, and Alex. Alex, a cop, was Micheal's best friend, they grew up together, worked on the force together. He was just as devastated by this whole mess as Trinity, and he often came by to check on her, and keep her company.

"Trinity, are you okay?" Sarah inquired, noticing her friend had that far away look in her eyes again.

"Huh? Yes, yes I am fine."

" I am going to stay over at Kev's tonight. Will you be alright?"

" I think I can manage. Go, go spend time with Kevin. Don't worry Sarah, I'll be fine sweetie. I plan on going to bed early anyways. So its not like I would have been much company."

"Okay, but..."

"*Sarah.*"

"All right, I am gone!" Sarah giggled as she headed for the door.

Trinity finished her tea, washed out the cup, and headed for her bedroom. She threw on her nightgown, and slid into bed. Thoughts of Micheal creeping into her mind, as she drifted off to sleep. *How she missed him.*

She could not move, could barely breathe with his weight atop her. She opened her mouth to scream, but nothing came out. Her limbs refused to move for her, she was paralyzed. Betrayed by her own body. Her nightgown was torn from her and discarded. Moonlight reflected off one long razor nail as it edged closer to her face........

Trinity woke with a start. Jerked from her slumber by the frightening images. Sweat dripping down her forehead, her breathing rapid and labored. *What a wretched nightmare.* It seemed so real, it took Trinity a few moments to realize there was no one in her room, and she was fine. She could've sworn she seen a man standing in her doorway. She heard something. Footsteps? Yes! There was definitely someone in her house. Trinity quietly slid out of bed and ran to the closet for the gun Micheal kept there. She peeked around the corner, *no one.* She put her back to the wall and crept toward the living room. *There!*

She saw him. She lifted the gun and pointed it in his direction...............

The living room light came on. " Whoa, don't shoot!" Alex said stretching his hands out in front him.

"Damn you Alex, I almost shot you!! You scared the hell out of me! What are you doing here?"

10

" Sarah called and asked if I'd stay over and keep an eye on you. She worries about you you know. Though, I am not sure why." Alex said, flashing her a grin while taking the gun from her hands and laying it on a nearby table.

"A little heads up would've been nice. You could be lying on my carpet right now bleeding to death." Trinity said as she followed Alex to the kitchen.

" I tried to phone, there was no answer. I got a little worried and came right over. That's when I found you sleeping like a baby. I was trying to be quiet so I didn't wake you." Alex said as he reached into the fridge and grabbed a bottle of wine.

" I could use a drink. You?" Alex asked.

"After the night I've had, I could use the bottle." Trinity said snickering as she grabbed two long stemmed glasses from the cabinet, and followed Alex to the couch. He was handsome in his uniform, the navy blue complimented his dark features. His hair was black as night, and his skin a natural bronze. His eyes, a deep vivid green, that stood out against his dark hair and skin. They reminded Trinity of cat's eyes. He had a strong jaw, and a sensuous smile. She'd always thought him appealing.

" Looked to me like you were having a pretty good night, snoozing away." Alex said as he filled their glasses, handing her one.

" I was, until I had this horrible nightmare, and then almost shot a guy." Trinity said teasingly, smiling at Alex and nudging him in the shoulder, nearly causing him to spill his wine.

"Easy now, I almost missed my mouth."Alex laughed, as he swallowed the last of the dark liquid and sat his glass on the coffee table to refill it.

After much conversation and an emptied bottle of wine, Trinity was ready to call it a night, and try to get some sleep. It was late and she was feeling the effects of their indulgence.

They went together, Sarah's room was right next to Trinity's.

" You can stay in Sarah's room, I'll see you in the morning. Good night Alex." Trinity said as she turned toward her bedroom.

"Trin...."

Alex said reaching out to grab her arm and turn her to face him. She was beautiful, scantily clad in her pink silken nightgown that fell just past her thighs. Her waist length blond hair falling across her shoulder, deep blue eyes staring into his. Alex could control himself no longer. He bent his head towards her, and connected with the soft pink flesh of her lips.

Trinity thought about stopping it, pushing him away, but only fleetingly.

It had been too long. She wrapped her arms around him and pulled him closer to her, deepening their kiss. Alex lifted her from the ground, and carried her into the bedroom.

"Good morning sleepy head." Alex said, as Trinity rolled over to face him, and opened her eyes. He had been watching her as she slept, thoughts of the nights events running through his mind. She looked so peaceful, like an angel. He had always been in love with Trinity. But, he dared not betray Micheal, he had been like a brother to him. He had always kept his feelings for her hidden. But now, Micheal was dead, and Trinity needed him. *Hell, he needed her.* He was hoping this wasn't happening to fast for her. He wanted to take it a little slower for her sake, after everything she's been through, but, he just wasn't sure if he could. Especially after last night. He'd half expected her to push him away. When she didn't, he lost all control of himself.

"Good morning." Trinity smiled sleepily, stretching her arms above her head. Alex was propped up on one elbow, looking at her. A sheet was laying across his waist, and the rest of his body bare. Trinity snuggled up against his bare chest, and he wrapped his arms around her. It felt good to be in his arms.

" Trinity....."

"No.... don't say anything, Alex. I just want to lay beside you for awhile."

"We have to talk about it eventually Trin."

Trinity sat up, bent her head toward him, and whispered against his lips,

"No words are necessary."

God she was beautiful. Alex pulled Trinity astride him, and the previous evening's encounter began anew.

Fully sated, Alex and Trinity decided it was time to get out of bed and start their day. Sarah had come home, and her and Kevin were in the kitchen. Trinity could smell the coffee brewing, and heard them talking. She quickly threw on her robe, brushed her teeth, and pulled her hair up. Alex dressed and followed her to the kitchen.

Sarah smiled wide at Trinity as she walked in with Alex following behind her, she flashed her a knowing wink. Trinity rolled her eyes, smiled, and headed for the coffee cups.

" Well, about time you two got up! Breakfast anyone? I made pancakes." Sarah knew Alex had spent the night, but she had no idea *where*, until she got home and her room was empty. *It's about time.* She thought. Trinity needed to get on with her life. And Alex was perfect for her. She'd known for years that Alex had a deep affection for her friend. She could see it in his eyes every time he looked at her. Sarah thought they made a good match.

" Sarah, your a girl after my own heart, I am starving!" Alex said, grabbing a plate and heading for the table where stacks of pancakes and bacon were waiting.

"I'll bet you are! Worked up an appetite did ya? " Kevin snickered, sitting down opposite Alex. Alex's grin revealed his speculations were right. Kevin nodded his head in approval.

" Wow, everything looks great Sarah. Thanks." Trinity said as she joined them at the table, setting a steaming cup of coffee in front of Alex.

"Thanks. It was definitely an interesting night....." Alex began, telling the story of how Trinity almost shot him, while everyone ate their breakfast.

Trinity and Alex had been seeing each other steadily for almost two months now. He asked her to move in with him, but she wasn't ready to leave her house yet. She'd put so much work into the place. Alex stayed with her every night he wasn't on duty. It had become like a second home to him. Sarah had recently moved in with Kevin, and Trinity decided to turn her old room into a studio. Trinity liked to paint, was pretty good at it too. She'd sold some of her work before, but had stopped painting after Micheal died. She was ready to paint again, missed it actually. She was beginning to feel more like her old self. She even started doing her own shopping and running her own errands. She actually started living again. The only thing that still haunts her are the horrific nightmares she has. They were coming more frequently now, and starting to take on a realism that chilled her bones. She scared Alex many nights, waking him from a dead sleep. He had been concerned at first, then just rationalized that it had to do with everything she had been through. It *had* been a crazy eight months. Her life was finally beginning to have some sort of normalcy to it.

Trinity was just finishing up dinner. Alex would be there any minute now. She wanted everything to be perfect. She sat the bottle of wine on the table, and lit the candles that sat in the center. She had planned a nice romantic dinner just for the two of them this evening. Sarah and Kevin usually joined them about three nights a week, but tonight, it was just going to be them.

"Trin!" Alex yelled from the living room as he came through the door.

"In the kitchen Alex."

Alex greeted her with a light kiss.

"Wow, this looks great!" Alex noticing all the work she'd done for their special evening.

The table was covered in a rich brown satin tablecloth, a runner lay across the center in the same fabric, only much lighter in color. Candles flickered in the center, reflecting their soft light off the crystal wine glasses and carefully placed silverware. The fine plate ware was adorned with an intricate design incorporating autumn leaves that perfectly matched the tablecloth. A bottle of wine sat chilling between their place settings. It was beautiful. *It was the perfect setting.*

"Thanks, I thought we'd have a nice dinner, just the two of us."

Alex reached into his pocket and dropped to one knee in front of Trinity. He opened the small velvet box to reveal the glittering diamond ring that lay nestled inside.

Trinity's eyes grew wide.

" Trin, I have loved you from the moment I met you. I want to spend the rest of my life with you. Will you do me the honor of becoming my wife?"

Trinity was shocked, she didn't see this one coming. She did love him. She'd known that for awhile. She hadn't told him that yet.

" Oh Alex, Yes!!" Trinity screamed, as Alex slid the ring onto her finger. He rose and kissed her, holding her for an extra moment. *She was going to be his wife.*

" You had me sweating there for a minute. I thought you were going to turn me down."

" Never. I love you Alex."

Alex smiled at the revelation. He couldn't believe he'd actually been afraid she didn't return his feelings. He kissed her again, and whispered against her lips,

"And I love you."

They sat down and enjoyed their first dinner together as a newly engaged couple. Both were blissfully aware their lives were about to change.

It was dark, the moonlight was barely visible through the heavy rain that crashed in steady waves outside the bedroom window. The only light that filtered in was an occasional lightning strike. Thunder rolled threateningly, not far in the distance.

He was there,

on top of her again. His foul breath smelled of death. Her nose burned from the pungent odor. She could not move. Her voice failed her, couldn't scream. She was helpless beneath him. Her nightgown torn from her body in shreds, and her panties ripped from her. A stream of crimson was flowing down her neck. She felt him moving within her as she bucked and writhed trying to escape him. It only seemed to excite him more.

Lightning.

His face no longer a dark blur, but vividly clear with the quick flash.

Micheal!!

Trinity let out a bloodcurdling scream, and Alex jumped to his feet, instinctively grabbing his gun off the nightstand. Almost as quickly, he realized Trinity had had another one of her nightmares. He put the gun back, crawled back into bed and wrapped his arms around her.

" It's okay baby. It was just a dream."

" Mi... Mi.... Micheal!" she managed through her tears.

" Oh god Trin. I'm sorry. I know. I miss him too." trying to console her.

16

Alex reached over and turned on the bedside lamp.

" Jesus! What the hell happened?!!" Alex not believing what he was seeing

.

Trinity was stark naked, her nightgown and panties torn and lying in the floor next to the bed. Blood ran down her cheek and neck from a scratch that started just under her cheekbone and ended at her jawline. Small droplets trickled from five scratches that ran from the side of her knee to her upper thigh. Her pillow stained with blood, and the sheet was spattered in the same crimson liquid. A flashback of past crime scene photos came flooding into Alex's mind.

" It... w-was... Micheal."

" She's okay. She's sleeping on the couch right now. Look, I have something I have to do. Can you come sit with her while I'm gone? It shouldn't take long .Great, Thanks."Alex hung up the phone, and went into the living room. He knelt down in front of the couch and caressed Trinity's cheek. She stirred.

" Trin, I have to run out for a few. I won't be gone long. Sarah should be here in just a few minutes."

Trinity nodded her head and closed her eyes. Alex kissed her forehead, and headed out the door for the station. He needed to find that case file.

Alex stared at the photos that were spread across his desk. He found it difficult to look at the pictures of Micheal, and he turned them face down. He had been right. The photos of the rape victim showed the exact same wounds as Trin's, only the victim's were much deeper. *But how was this possible?* Micheal was dead. He could not have done it. *None of this was making any damn sense.* Alex thought, as he scooped up the photos and placed them back inside in the file. Was it possible that Trinity was doing this to herself? *Surely not.* He'd known how hard the circumstances surrounding Micheal's death had been on her, but the girl wasn't capable of such an act. Did Micheal have a partner? Had he been inside the house, right there under his nose? He didn't think someone could get in or out of the house without him noticing, but, Alex couldn't be sure of anything right now. *Something was happening, and he was damn sure going to find out what it was.* His officer's instincts were on high alert. He needed to talk to Sarah. He put the file away and headed back to Trinity's.

Trinity was still sleeping. Sarah and Kevin sat at the kitchen table sipping a cup of coffee, when Alex walked in.

" What the hell happened here last night Alex?" Kevin asked. He had decided to come with Sarah. She had been afarid to go alone after Alex told her what happened. She was afraid someone might still be in the house, or worse, come back. She'd tried to explain to Kevin what she'd been told, but he could not quite grasp it.

" It's a long story. I fill you in on the details shortly. But first, I need to ask you guys a few questions." Alex began his inquiry into Trinity's recent state of mind, leading into the events of last night, and ending with the discovery he'd made after viewing the crime scene photos.

" You can't possibly think she would do this to herself,do you?" Sarah asked Alex, giving him a look that should have sent him running for the nearest exit. But he never faltered from her gaze.

" No, I don't." He said, "I know her better than that. I was only asking if you think Micheal's death is the cause of these nightmares of hers."

"Well, she's had them since his funeral."Sarah offered.

" I think they are not only caused by Micheal's death, but it is Micheal himself." Kevin suggested, after carefully going over the happenings in his mind.

Alex and Sarah both staring at him in confusion.

" Okay, before you two lock either one of us up in the nut house, let me explain." Kevin said pointing at himself and Trinity still sleeping soundly.

" Have you ever heard of an *Incubus*?"

Blank stares.

" An incubus is a demon of sorts, it visits women in their dreams. There have been cases reported of women who have encountered them. They were beaten, scratched, bruised, and even raped by such demons. Most of which had marks that look similar to the ones on Trinity's body. I think Micheal has returned from the grave as an incubus, here for one last conquest. *Trinity*." Kevin explained.

"'You can't be serious, Kevin. A demon? Returned from the grave?" Alex laughed at the ridiculous notion.

" I'm serious. My advice to you would be to get Trinity out of this house. As long as she's here, he *will* find her. Next time, he may even *kill* her."

" He's right Alex. The best thing *is* to get her *out* of here. Demon or no, this place holds too many memories. That alone could be contributing to her problem." Sarah said.

" You don't really believe this do you?" Alex asked Kevin.

" I think anything is possible. There are a lot of things we still do not understand about the world, or even ourselves. Look, I am no expert, but, I did a paper on the paranormal, and paranormal events in college for a Psychology class. You'd be surprised how much information you retain after weeks of research."

Alex wasn't sure he was buying this new explanation. He was leaning more towards Micheal having an accomplice. He just had to figure out how to catch the bastard.

" On a more positive note," Alex said as Trinity walked into the kitchen," guess who got engaged last night." Trinity smiled, and held out her hand for Sarah to see the large diamond engagement ring that rested comfortably on her finger.

" I'm so happy for you guys!" Sarah squealed, and hugged her.

" Thanks. We are excited too. We aren't rushing to set a date yet." Trinity said.

" No, we want to take our time." Alex agreed.

" Congrats!!" Kevin said. " We must celebrate, tonight!.."

" That's a great idea Kev. I'll make dinner for you guys, here tonight, we'll have some wine, it'll be great!" Sarah offered, planning to spend the night in case Trinity needed her.

" Sounds like a plan." Alex said smiling at Trinity, who nodded in agreement. His eyes tracing the long scratch that lined her face. His determination renewed to find the person responsible.

Trinity was glad for the company, it had been a good night. She enjoyed having dinner with her friends. Sarah, as always made her forget her troubles for awhile. They had just finished cleaning up the kitchen, and Kevin and Alex had just readied the couch bed.

" Good night guys." Trinity said as her and Alex headed off to bed. Kevin turned off the lights, and flipped the TV on, as Sarah crawled into the bed and curled up against him.

Once again trinity was in the midst of a horrific nightmare, as she tossed and bucked trying to fight him off. Alex awoke to an unimaginable sight. A manlike beast on top of Trinity, his claws like razors digging deep into her flesh as he shredded the nightgown from her body. He turned to look at Alex,

Micheal's face!

Alex sobered immediately realizing he was not dreaming. He grabbed his gun and fired. *Nothing.*

" Leave her alone Micheal! She doesn't belong to you anymore!" Alex taunted the beast.

The bullet passed through its body and embedded itself in the far wall of the bedroom.

The beast let out an ear-piercing roar, and lunged at him. Trinity awoke at the sound of the gunshot.

A scream.

At the same time Kevin and Sarah came bursting through the bedroom door, and stopped dead in their tracks.

Another scream.

The demon lunged with razor nails stretched out at Alex, missing him by inches. Then turned its attention back to Trinity. He leaped toward her, razor sharp nails stretched, determined to hit their mark.

Alex fired again.

Kevin reached over and turned on the bedroom light,

the beast was gone, disappearing with the darkness.

Alex ran to Trinity holding her protectively against him. Kevin hugged Sarah and held her tight as they each tried to rationalize in their own minds what had just occurred.

" Well, this is the last box. " Trinity said as she handed it off to Alex to load into the moving truck.

" Great! That's it then. You ready?"

Trinity turned to look at the house one last time, *so many memories. Some of which she was glad to leave behind.*

" Yeah," she said, smiling at Alex as she got in the passenger side of the truck. " I think I am."

Alex reached over and held her hand as they pulled away. He was glad she finally decided to move in with him. He glanced into the rear view mirror as the house faded into the distance, and smiled, knowing that he had won . Micheal would never hurt her again.

For Sale By Owner ©2007

It was a warm summer's morning, not too hot yet, when Bailey awoke. She thought it a perfect day for her and her husband Chris, to go house hunting. The newlyweds had been living with Chris's parents for months. They were more than ready to be out on their own. Bailey just had not found the right place yet. She wanted something a little old fashioned, maybe an old farm house that she and Chris could fix up themselves. She wanted something they could make their own, and something big enough for any future children. Bailey would know the right place when she seen it. They had been looking for a place, unsuccessfully, for weeks now. She did not mean to be so picky, but this is a place where she was going to spend the rest of her life with Chris, and raise their children. It could be no less than *perfect*. Today was the day, she could feel it. Excited, Bailey hurriedly put on a pot of coffee, and headed for the shower.

" Bailey, honey, you have got to decide on something. We are running out of options here. We've been looking at houses for weeks. You had to have seen something you liked." Chris pleaded, as he and Bailey were driving over to view their last house for the day.

They had already seen four, and Chris was getting a little aggravated that Bailey could not make up her mind. He was anxious to get out of his parents' house, and actually start living like a normal married couple. Chris's parents were pretty old fashioned in their thinking, and he and Bailey had been sleeping in separate rooms for months. They had to sneak into one another's rooms after his parents went to sleep. He felt like a fucking teenager again for god's sake. It was getting tiresome.

" I am sorry Chris. I can't help myself. I just want everything to be perfect. I liked a few of the places we've seen, they just didn't feel right. They were just lacking that little something, ya know. " Just then, as she was staring out the passenger window, Bailey saw it. It was perfect!

"Chris! Stop! Pull over right here! Would you look at that."

It was a large plantation home. White, with large columns along the front. It sat in the middle of about 20 acres of land, and there were cows grazing in the distance. A graying old barn sat in a far field with hay bales stacked against one side, and to the other side a large pond glistened in the summer afternoon sun. There were three magnolia trees in the front of the house, each with a swing hanging from one of their branches. The back was completely surrounded by a rainbow of different colored flowers, bushes, and young flowering trees. A single stone pathway led into the back garden from the large veranda on the side of the house. A two foot fence surrounded the garden and the entire back length of the house, white, picket. It really was perfect.

" This place? Haven't you heard the locals gossiping about this house.?"

"You know I don't care to listen to gossip Chris. The locals are a bunch of old busybodies, with nothing better to do with their time. I don't see a *for sale* sign."

"They say that the family who lives here is really weird. They're kids only come out to play at night."

" Well, maybe they have an allergy to sunlight. There are actually a lot of people who do, you know." Bailey said, bummed because there was no for sale sign.

" Well, so much for that idea. It would have been so perfect. But, obviously, its not for sale. Lets head on over to the last house. Maybe it will be the one." Bailey said, knowing she'd already found her house, and yet, she was still looking.

" I am sorry sweetie. We'll find *our* perfect home. I promise." Chris said as he reached across the seat to hold her hand, and Bailey stared longingly into the side view mirror, watching her dream home fade into the distance.

The sun had set only an hour ago, and the veranda was lit with the soft light that flowed from the many candles lining the railing. Several more sat atop the table where Brynn and her husband Ron sat sipping a crimson liquid from their wine glasses, watching their daughters play on the swings. Three more glasses sat empty atop the table, awaiting their fill. It was still quite warm, a light breeze occasionally came through to relieve the heat. The half moon shone bright floating in the blue-black sky above. The girls' silken white gowns captured an occasional moonbeam, reflecting from the soft fabric every time a swing peeked out from under the trees. Brynn always loved to dress the girls in white, and pull their hair up in pigtails with silken bows tied around to match. It made them look *angelic*. She preferred wearing black herself, as did Ron.

" Ron, what do you think we should do about the girls? They are complaining more and more every day. They're starving."

" I think they should be happy with what they have. They are rather spoiled, ya know. You have always had a problem refusing them anything. As far as I am concerned they can eat what we eat." Ron stated, capturing Brynn's deep blue-gray eyes.

Brynn had always given in to Jesslynn, Danicka, and Kira's demands. She really should be more authoritive with the girls. Ron felt as if they took advantage of their mother sometimes. Knowing she could deny them no request. He loved his girls, kill for them, but they needed more discipline if they were going to survive in their world.

"They don't like the taste. You know what they crave, as do we all." Brynn said as she rose from the table and went inside the house.

She returned in seconds holding a small dagger, its intricately jeweled hilt and blade reflecting the candlelight.

" I think we should put the house up for sale, honey."

" You love this house Brynn, why are you going to sell it?" Ron asked.

" I'm not ." Brynn said as she walked over to the calf who was tied up on the other side of the veranda. It let out a loud yelp as the dagger was plunged deep into the flesh of its neck, severing its jugular. Brynn filled the three empty glasses nearly overflowing with the warm crimson liquid.

"Girls! Dinner!"

8 P.M., there was a knock on the door. It was their first showing, and Brynn was excited. Two weeks had passed since she put the house in the newspaper and hung her signs. *Finally* someone was interested. The young couple had phoned earlier in the week to set up a time to view the inside of the house. Brynn had explained that she and her husband worked very late, and could only do showings in the evenings.

" Hello, come in." Brynn said as she opened the door for her guests.

" Hi, I am Auron, and this is my wife Alicia. We absolutely love the property. We're ready to see the house." He said as they exchanged handshakes.

" Trust me, you will never set eyes on a place like this again." Brynn smiled, as she lead them through the foyer, into the great room, the den, dining room, and kitchen. The house boasted hardwood floors throughout, beautifully maintained, with a slick shine. A huge staircase and balcony overlooked the great room. A crystal chandelier hung from the ceiling reflecting prismic lights that danced on the slick hardwood below.

"This place is absolutely gorgeous!" Alicia squealed.

'Thanks, are you ready to see the upstairs? It has the only carpet in the house. There are four bedrooms, and three and a half baths upstairs. Plenty of closet space in the master, with the *his* and *hers* walk-ins. I am sorry its a little dark up here, we have several blown bulbs I meant to change before you arrived. But it is beautiful in the candlelight." Brynn explained as she led them up the grand staircase.

Jesslyn, Danicka, and Kira were lying in wait, counting the approaching footsteps. Just as they saw their mother pass their room, in unison they lunged.......................

swooping in on their prey. Their little fangs hitting their mark deep within the flesh of Auron's neck. Droplets of blood landing on the gray carpet, from the crimson streams running down their newly saturated white gowns. They were quickly draining his strength, and Auron dropped to the floor, unable to fight the young vampires off. Brynn grabbed Alicia as the girl released a bloodcurdling scream, and tried to run. She drug her into the bedroom where Ron was waiting. She threw her onto the bed and climbed atop her to hold her down. Brynn leaned in and nipped the girl's lip, licking the droplets of blood from the small tear in the soft flesh. Then she smiled wickedly, bearing her fangs to the frightened Alicia.

Ron thought it arousing, seeing Brynn astride the young girl, holding her there for him against the deep red satin coverlet on the bed. His hunger for more than blood was fierce, demanding. Brynn reading the fire that burned in her husband's eyes, ripped the girls blouse from her, exposing her full round breast. Ron bent to caress the struggling girl's cheek. He smiled in satisfaction as he cupped the mound in his strong hand, kissed the girl's now swollen lips, and sunk his teeth deep into the creamy white flesh of her neck. After Ron had his fill, she would finish her.

Bailey had finally decided on a house. Her and Chris were on their way to close the deal now. It wasn't her idea of perfect, but, she decided they could make anything work. She just had to take it one project at a time.

" I am so excited! We are going to have our own place, finally, we can be alone!"

"Yeah," said Chris, " and we can share a bed!" they laughed. Chris giving Bailey a playful wink.

Bailey glanced out the passenger window,

" Chris look!! *Oh my god,* stop the car!!"

Chris pulled the car to the side of the road, and they got out. He looked up to see the old plantation house with three swings hanging from the branches of three magnolia trees.

Bailey's perfect house.

"Look, its *fate!*" Bailey exclaimed.

Chris looked in the direction Bailey was pointing, directly at a huge sign in the yard that read,

FOR SALE BY OWNER.

Little Girl Lost ©2007

"Carrie?"

"Carrie, did you hear me?" Tara asked, gently nudging her daughter in the shoulder to get the child's attention. She was concerned finding Carrie lying on her bed staring wide-eyed daydreaming, *again*.

" Huh?" Carrie asked, suddenly being pulled back into reality.

" I said , its time for you to get cleaned up. We are having company over for dinner tonight."

" Okay mommy. Who's coming over?"

" Aunt Niki and the kids........and Carrie, I really wish you would find something better to do with your time. It isn't healthy for a 10 year old girl to stay locked away in her bedroom all day reading and daydreaming. Girls your age need sunshine and fresh air. Why don't you go outside and make some new friends. I see kids in the neighborhood about your age all the time. I know the move has been hard sweetie. But, its gonna be great, you just have to give it a chance." Tara suggested as she left Carrie's room, and headed for the kitchen to get started on preparations for the nights dinner.

 She often wondered what exactly it was Carrie spent all her time daydreaming about. It worried her sometimes how withdrawn Carrie had become since her father bailed on them two years ago, and the recent move had only made matters worse. Sometimes Tara found herself wishing Tim was still around, but he hadn't had much to do with them since he ran off with his secretary. It had been a bitter divorce. Tim got the house, and in exchange she got sole custody of Carrie. All Carrie got from her father were the measly child support payments that show up in the mail every month. Some father he turned out to be. It was difficult being a single working mother, but she was managing. Thank god for Niki, her sister has been a real help to her through all of this mess. They were finally getting their lives back on track, all except for Carrie's solitude. Maybe it was just a phase, and she would outgrow it. It will pass, Tara thought.

Carrie loved spending time with her cousins, and Aunt Niki. It was the only time she really wanted to play anymore. She missed her daddy. She missed her old house, and her friends, even more. The new house was okay, it was a lot smaller than Carrie was used to. But, she did like her new room. It was upstairs, almost the whole top floor, aside from the bathroom. She had a bay window that overlooked the front street. Sometimes Carrie would sit there and watch the neighborhood kids play ball. But, most of the time that was her favorite reading spot. She been reading a lot of books lately, especially on her new favorite subject, *Astral Projection*. Carrie was glad dinner was over and Aunt Niki and the kids went home. She was ready to be alone again. She hurriedly donned her favorite nightgown, white, that fell to her ankles, with pink lace trim on the neck and sleeves. She turned down her cover, and slid into bed. Carrie flipped on the over head reading lamp, and grabbed her favorite book that lay hidden just underneath her pillow.

Tara awoke to the alarm buzzing in her ears, and hit the snooze button, *she'd thought*. She had accidentally turned it off and had overslept, now they were going to be running late. She hurriedly dressed in her waitress's uniform and readied herself for another grueling day at the diner. Carrie would be late for school if she did not pick up the pace a bit.

Tara quickly went upstairs to wake Carrie. Carrie's bedside lamp was still on, and she was sitting up in her bed, staring wide-eyed at her when she entered her room.

" Carrie, get up and get dressed. You're going to be late for school, and I am going to be late for work. Bob said if I was late one more time he was going to fire me. Hurry."

Tara said as she pulled a light pink dress from a clothes hanger in Carrie's closet, and dug through the carpeted floor to find her matching pink sandals . " Carrie?" No answer.

"Carrie,....did you....."

She turned to look at Carrie, pink cloth and shoes falling to the floor with a thud, as she rushed to her daughter's bedside. "Carrie!!!"

" Ms. Sanders?" the doctor interrupted Tara's frantic pacing, which she had been doing for hours since arriving with Carrie at the ER.

"Yes,..?" Tara said , turning to face the doctor, wiping at her tear stained cheeks.

" Ms. Sanders, I have good news, and bad news. We have done every single test known to man. There is nothing *medically* wrong with your daughter. All her vital functions are perfect. According to these test results, she's a perfectly healthy 10 year old. Yet, she is still unresponsive. She isn't responding to external stimuli, light, sound, or even touch. She does not blink, talk, or move. She remains in a vegetative state."

" What?... So your telling me you have no idea what is wrong with her?" Tara wasn't sure she was understanding what was being told to her.

" Well, yes, and no ma'am. I am telling you there is nothing *medically* wrong with Carrie. But, I do have an idea of what her problem may be. Has she ever had a psychiatric evaluation, or recently been under the care of a psychiatrist?"

" What!? Are you saying my daughter's crazy?! That this is all in her head or she's pretending?!" Tara could not believe her ears. She knew things had been rough for them lately, but there was nothing wrong with Carrie. She was a perfectly normal girl. What the hell was he talking about!?

" I am sorry ma'am, I was not trying to insult you. I am trying to tell you that myself, or any one else here at this hospital can not help your daughter. She needs to be evaluated by a psychiatrist. I have already called ahead and made arrangements. They are on the way to transport her now. This is a highly reputable facility, and they specialize in conditions such as Carrie's. They should be arriving shortly. I am sorry, but, they will better be able to help your daughter."

And with that the doctor was gone, leaving Tara staring bewildered after him.

A psychiatric hospital? Tara felt her world was beginning to spin violently out of control.

Carrie had stood helpless, watching her panic-stricken mother as she'd carried her body downstairs to the car and drove away. She'd tried to tell her not to cry, that she was okay. She was right there beside her, holding her hand, and trying to comfort her. But her mother could not hear, feel, or see her. She stood now staring out her window, waiting.

Carrie had been practicing astral projection for months now. She loved the feeling of freedom it gave her. A peace she had never known came over her as she explored the astral world. Each time she would travel further, to explore the great cities of times past, and farther beyond the stars and the planets into the great abyss of darkness and light. She loved to fly to the moon, and turn and gaze upon the earth, or soar along the oceans, and watch the dolphins follow her below the water's surface. Each time she was able to return to her body. This time, Carrie had strayed too far, stayed away too long. She found her body, but had been unable to reunite with it. She was trapped outside, her soul suspended in another dimension.

It had been two years since Carrie had developed her condition. Carrie had spent a year in the psych ward. The doctors had given up after months of different therapies and medications had failed to improve Carrie's condition. They had wanted to send her to a convalescent, but Tara had refused, and took Carrie home. She had to quit her job at the diner, and found part time work at a local drug store in the evenings. Niki cared for Carrie while Tara was working, Tim had only seen her once, and never came back. Although, he had been paying Carrie's medical bills. Tara would be in a world of trouble if he hadn't. She could barely keep a roof over their heads. It had been an endless nightmare for almost a year now. She thought she would go over the edge when doctors told her Carrie needed a feeding tube inserted. It was heart wrenching to watch her day in and day out just lying there, with her eyes wide open, always staring, never blinking, never moving, *nothing*. Tara had a hard time coping, and had been seeing a therapist herself. He prescribed her antidepressants. Although they didn't seem to help her mood much, she took them anyway. She also began taking sleeping pills with her nightly glass of wine, to help with the nightmares. She would often dream that Carrie would come into her room while she was sleeping, stand at the foot of her bed and call to her. *Mommy, I am okay*, she would say. *Don't cry. I am right here, here with you.* And, just as Tara would reach out to her, she was gone. Tara would wake only to find Carrie in the same state of nothingness, which only sent her spiraling anew, deeper into her depression.

The nightmares were coming more frequently now, and Tara was having more than one glass of wine with her pills at night. The combination left her feeling irritable and groggy in the mornings. Making her day's work caring for Carrie even more difficult than normal. She did not feel like herself anymore. Sometimes she wished she could just go to sleep, and never wake up. She no longer clung to the hope that Carrie would recover. She finally realized that this was her life, it was the way it was. There was no changing it. She finished off her bottle of wine, and downed a couple of sleeping pills. She would give Carrie her bath, then go on to bed herself.

Tara was feeling the effects of the wine as she ran Carrie's bath. She carefully lifted Carrie into the tub, and began soaping her washcloth. Tears fell silently as Tara bathed her daughter. She just did not know how much longer she could go on living like this. What had happened to her life? Everything used to be so wonderful, at one time, they had everything. Now, they do not even have each other.

Carrie stood beside her mother, and placed her hand on her shoulder. *I am here mommy, I am here with you. Don't cry. I am okay.* But, as always her mother could not hear her, and she could not see her. The only time she could was late at night when she would go into her mother's room. Sometimes she would crawl in bed with her and lay beside her all night. She missed her mother's hugs and kisses. Missed her touch. She wanted so badly to be back in her own body again. She'd tried and tried, and just could not do it. Carrie watched as Tara bathed her body.

"Forgive me baby, I love you always." Tara whispered into Carrie's ear, as she reached over and turned the tub water back on.

Mommy, what are you doing?

Tara slowly pushed Carrie's head under the water that was now flowing over the side of the tub in flooding waves, to the tiled floor below.

Mommy no! Stop!

Carrie was afraid, trying to pull her mother away from her body, astonished at what she saw. To no avail. Her hand slid completely through her mother's body to the other side. Carrie was helpless, she could only watch in horror.

Tara sobbed uncontrollably as she held her daughter's head under the water, watching the air bubbles from her nose float to the surface and disappear, her eyes staring wide, unblinking, right at Tara.

Mommy ,please don't. Please!! Carrie reached down to pull herself from the tub. She did not want to die. She grabbed at her lifeless hand...................

Carrie blinked, jerked.

Horrified, Tara let go.

Coughing and sputtering, through tears, obvious fear in her little eyes,

"Mommy!! ...please......" Carrie managed through the water that was ejected from her mouth and nose, as she was suddenly reunited with her body.

Tara crawled across the bathroom floor mumbling incoherently through her tears. She sat in the corner with her back to the wall, and hugged her knees to her chest. Carrie rose from the tub, and walked over to her mother, gently laying her hand on the woman's shoulder caressing her comfortingly.

" I am here. I am here with you. Don't cry, mommy. I am okay."

" Mommy?" Carrie asked, as she knelt down to look at her mother.

" *Mommy*!?"

Tara sat, staring wide-eyed, unblinking, and unmoving...............

Mara ©2007

Caleb was ready, another night on the town, another woman in his bed.
He wasn't the *settling down* type of guy. At least, not yet. He was
having too much fun playing the field. He and his buddies, Shane and
Ryan, were headed over to a bar that had just recently opened,*Club
Shadows*. They'd heard it was a happening place, full of beautiful
women ripe for the plucking, and they were going to try their luck.
The guys have an on-going bet, that whoever sleeps with the sexiest
woman, pays everybody else's way the following weekend. Most of the
time Caleb won. He was reigning champ six weeks in a row, now. He
was determined not to lose his title tonight, and was scanning the
crowded nightclub for the best choice.

" So, who's the *not-so-lucky* lady tonight Caleb?" Shane asked him,
scanning the crowd himself.

" Bingo!" Ryan said, as he headed for the bar, where a woman sat with
her back to them, her long night-black hair falling nearly to the floor.

Caleb and Shane watched as Ryan approached the woman. He offered
her a drink which she accepted. When the bartender handed her the
drink, she proceeded to pour it over Ryan's head. Having struck out,
Ryan returned to stand beside Caleb and Shane. They were laughing
hysterically at Ryan's misfortune, while he was wiping his face with a
bar towel.

" *Shut up*. You think you can do any better, go for it. She's an evil
one!" Ryan said laughing at himself.

" I accept that challenge." Caleb said. " *Watch* and *learn*!" he said as
he handed his mug of beer over to Shane.

Caleb walked over to the bar where the woman was still sitting. He was surprised as she stood up to greet him. She was tall, but not overly so. She had thick black hair that fell past her thighs, and extremely light blue eyes. Caleb had never seen eyes like hers. So alluring, they seem to draw you into their depth, and hold you prisoner there. She was well built, an hourglass shape, but not thick. She had thick full lips, and an ample bosom. How Caleb would love to wrap that hair around his fingers while,........*damn she was gorgeous.*

Ryan and Shane watched as Caleb weaved his spell over yet another unknowing beauty. The woman smiled at Caleb and took his hand, as they headed straight for them.

" See ya later,..... boys. " she said smiling seductively, as her and Caleb passed them, and headed for the exit. Caleb flashed them an " *I told you so*" grin, and then they disappeared from the nightclub, hand-in-hand.

" *No fucking way, man*! How the hell does he do that?!" Ryan, not believing he'd lost out to Caleb again.

" I *don't* know. Well, I guess we're footing the bill next weekend too . We might as well have another drink, I guess Caleb's gonna be awhile." Shane said shaking his head and grinning.

He figured Caleb could do it, he's always had a way with women. He had an unexplainable charm that drew women to him, ever since their college days. Shane had lost many competitions to Caleb too. But, he'd rather lose them. He had actually developed a conscience over the years, and preferred not to join in Ryan and Caleb's games. But, old habits die hard, and he found his self between a rock and a hard place when the guys started ribbing him over it. They said he'd gone soft, that he was a *pussy*. Thank god he could use his girlfriend, Melissa as an excuse not to join in now. He felt so bad for those girls. Caleb only used them. He slept with them, and tossed them away like garbage. It kinda made him sick. But, Caleb was his best friend. They were like brothers, inseparable. Besides, he did not know any of those women personally. He and Ryan grabbed up the nearest table, and ordered another round.

Caleb and Mara had arrived at his apartment only a few moments ago. Mara sat on the couch watching Caleb as he poured two shots of vodka, and walked over to hand her one. Mara sat hers on the table, as Caleb swallowed his down in one gulp.

" I am not in the mood to play subtle games." Mara started as she stood up and stared deep into Caleb's brown eyes, and pressing her breasts hard against him.

" I want you, Caleb." She whispered in his ear, running her hand up the inside of his thigh.

Caleb was slightly taken aback by her boldness, but was intrigued by it as well. He wasn't used to women taking control. He usually had be the one to do it. *God, but she was beautiful.* Caleb felt his self being drawn to her, unable to pull himself away. He bent his head towards hers, and kissed her deeply. She grabbed him by the hands and half dragged him onto the couch. She pushed him onto his back and straddled him, her black skirt sliding up to her hips, exposing her bare buttocks. Caleb grabbed her bottom and pressed her hard into him. She broke away from his lips as she reached to turn off the lamp. Mara quickly undressed and climbed atop Caleb again. She licked at his lips, and earlobe, and ran her tongue across his neck. She took one button from his shirt between her teeth and ripped it loose. Then, another, and another.

" Ow! Careful there!" Caleb said as he felt her teeth dig into the skin of his chest.

Mara licked at the droplets of blood that slowly crept from the scratches, then ripped his shirt completely from his body and promptly discarded it. She ran her long nails up the inside of his thighs, and unzipped his pants. Caleb quickly shed them and tossed them aside, along with his underwear. *It was his turn.* He spread a blanket from the back of the couch onto the floor, and Mara sat down on it. Caleb pushed Mara onto her back and positioned himself between her thighs. He drove hard into her, as Mara growled and bit deep into the flesh of his shoulder. Caleb groaned at the mix of pain and pleasure, trying to drive himself deeper within her. Mara ran her long nails down his back taking skin with them, as she suckled the blood running from Caleb's shoulder. Mara pushed Caleb onto his back again,climbed on, and rode him hard into a feverish climax.

Fully sated, she lay beside him tracing the scratches on his chest with her fingers, as he drifted into an exhausted sleep.

Caleb awoke to find Mara had already gone. He winced from the pain in his shoulder. He laid his hand across it and found it was still bleeding. Caleb headed for the bathroom. He was surprised at his reflection in the mirror. There was blood smeared across his lips and face, and he had long scratches down his back and chest, along with teeth marks. The wound on his shoulder was pretty deep, and dried blood ran down his arm and chest, with a few fresh crimson droplets making their way to the surface. She'd bitten into him hard. He looked like something from a horror film. *Damn that girl was a wild one.* Caleb thought, as he proceeded to clean himself up, and headed out to find Shane and Ryan.

Caleb found Shane and Ryan waiting outside the club, it had closed its doors only a few minutes ago. He picked them up and was headed over to drop them off at their apartment.

" Sounds like you had a hell of a night." Shane said after hearing about his friend's encounter with Mara.

" Yeah, I guess you could say that."Caleb replied, grinning.

" Damn, you *lucky* bastard. Wish I could find me a wildcat!" Ryan said, obviously jealous he wasn't the one to take Mara home. He'd struck out all night, although he had managed to pick up a couple of phone numbers. *Well, it was a start*, he thought.

" All right guys, I'll see you next weekend! You're paying!!" Caleb said as he dropped the guys off in front of their apartment building.

" See ya Champ!! You better enjoy your title this week. Cuz next week *you're going down*!!" Ryan said as they exited the car and waved Caleb

off. Caleb only laughed, as he drove away, heading for home, and his bed. It was late, and he was exhausted. *Not to mention sore as hell*. Thoughts of Mara returning to him.

She was astride him. Her long silken mane wrapped within his fingers as he pulled her hips to him, moving deeper within her. She bent down and flicked his lower lip with her tongue, and bit it slightly. Caleb opened his eyes wide in horror. A female-like creature was on top of him. She laughed evilly, exposing fangs dripping a thick crimson liquid that ran in streams from her mouth to her breasts. A horn loomed ominously out from under her thick black hair on either side of her head. Great bat-like wings protruded from the bluish-gray skin of her back and her long claw-like nails were bathed in blood. Her eyes matched the pale blue-gray of her skin. She wrapped her clawed fingers around his throat, as she continued to sate her demon lust upon him. He felt like she was cutting off his oxygen, as her claws dug dangerously into his flesh.

Caleb jerked, jumped from his bed and turned on the overhead light.

Damn!!

That was one of the worst nightmare's he'd ever experienced. It felt so real, almost like it was really happening. Drenched in sweat, his breathing fast and labored, his hands went instinctively to his throat. It felt as if someone actually had tried to strangle him. His throat and neck were extremely sore. He ran to the bathroom mirror. " *Nothing.* He could see no visible marks around his throat, or anywhere else, other than those left by his encounter with Mara. *He was losing it. It was just a damn dream.* He thought, dismissing it quickly. Then he headed back to his bed to try to rescue some of the precious few hours of sleep he had left.

It had been three weeks since Caleb met Mara at *Club Shadows*. His scratches had healed, but his shoulder hadn't. It was still tender and it burned like hell's fire. He'd been spending his week nights fighting off his damned nightmares, and his weekends searching for Mara who seemed to have fallen off the face of the earth. He hadn't seen or heard from her since the night they met. No one who worked at the club seemed to know her. Caleb was captivated by her, completely infatuated. He couldn't stop thinking about her. He wanted to see her again, wanted to be with her again. He had not slept with another woman since he'd been with her. He lost his title to Ryan the very next weekend, and he didn't care. There was only one woman on *his* mind. *Mara.*

Shane was happy for his friend. He had noticed the change in him immediately. He knew Caleb was in love, whether Caleb knew it or not. He also knew it would take one hell of a woman to take Caleb away from his bachelor's life. Shane just hadn't realized how right he was. She seemed to disappear into thin air. Caleb went to Club Shadows every weekend and sat at a table watching the door. Hoping she would be the next one in the club. So far, she hadn't made an appearance. They were headed back there now, and he hoped, for his friend's sake, that Mara would be there. He hated seeing the disappointment on Caleb's face.

Caleb sat at what had become his usual table, it had a bird's eye view of the front door. This time though, he decided to sit with his back to the door, that way he wasn't constantly staring at everyone who walked in. He ordered a shot of vodka and a mug of beer, and the same for Shane. Shane pulled up a chair in front of him and sat down.

" So Caleb, who's the not-so-lucky lady tonight ?" He grinned.

Caleb flashed him a go-to-hell look.

" Sorry man. I was just trying to cheer you up! It's not my fault your in love with a woman who vanished after you slept with her." Shane said jokingly.

In love? What the hell gave him that idea? *Was he*? Na, no way. They'd only been together one night. Caleb swallowed his shot down in one gulp, and chased it with half of his beer.

" Whoa! Slow down there buddy. You'll be down for the count in no time if you keep that up. I don't feel like carrying you outta here tonight, man." Shane laughed.

" You won't have to. Ryan can. " he said as he caught sight of Ryan across the bar flirting shamelessly with a little blond.

" Caleb......" Shane said pointing toward the door behind him. Caleb quickly turned his head in that direction. *It was her.* Mara.

Caleb smiled at her as she walked toward his table....and then kept right on walking over to a barstool, and sat down.

What the? Caleb looked over at Shane who shrugged his shoulders.

" Did you see that? She walked right past me."

"I don't know, man. Maybe ya scared her off."

" Well, I am going to find out ." Caleb said as he pushed his chair back and walked over to Mara.

" Mara?" Caleb asked as she turned to look at him. That was the moment it hit him, as he stared into her beautiful face. *He was in love with her. Good God, how the hell did that happen?* She did seem a little different, her eyes were darker than he'd thought.

" Do I know you?" Mara asked, not believing this devilishly handsome stranger knew her name. He was tall, with dark brown hair and brown eyes, and skin almost the same hue as his eyes. Striking, *sexy* even, he had those kind of eyes that beckoned a woman to do things she normally wouldn't.

" You don't recognize me? We were here together three weeks ago, remember?" Caleb asked, astonished that she really did not know who he was.

That had never happened to him before. Sure, he'd pulled that play on a few girls himself, he just couldn't believe it was being reciprocated. What a jerk he had been. He hadn't realized until just this moment, that he may have actually hurt someone in the process. He could've made them feel the way he was feeling right this moment.

" No, I don't think so. This is the first time I have ever been to this club. You must be mistaking me for someone else." Mara said, bewildered that this guy thought he knew her. But he couldn't, she'd never seen him before in her life.

" All right, Mara. I got it. I'll leave you alone." with that Caleb turned and walked away from her, past Shane, and right out the door, disappearing into the cool night air. Leaving Mara staring after him in complete confusion.

" Caleb, wait!" Shane yelled after him. He didn't even acknowledge Shane had spoken, just kept walking. He got outside in just enough time to see Caleb speeding off. *Damn. What the hell just happened?*

Shane went back inside to approach Mara.

" Jesus, Mara! What the hell did you say to him?"

" Excuse me? " Mara asked, looking up at yet another handsome stranger. " Who? What are you talking about? Do I know you?" *This was one strange club, full of wackos.* Mara thought.

Shane couldn't believe it. She was actually pretending not to know them.

" Damn it Mara!!Stop playing with him. Can't you see Caleb is in love with you!?" Shane said, as he turned to go after Caleb, and left the club.

" What the hell is going on? Can somebody please tell me what the hell is going on around here?" She did not know these people, yet they knew her. *And what in the world were they talking about?* Who is Caleb? Could he be that first handsome stranger? It had to be. In love with her? She did not even know him, he did not know her. Mara was thoroughly confused.

" I don't have a clue, but maybe you should've gotten their phone numbers. " Sylvia said. Mara's friend had been watching and listening to the whole charade. It had been very amusing. She wished guys would be more creative like that when they tried to pick her up. It would be so much more fun.

"Did you know those guys?"

" No."

"How did they know your name? "

" I have no idea. Maybe they overheard us talking." Mara offered.

" Probably, but, ya gotta admit. That's one of the best pick up attempts I have ever seen. They were such *cuties*!!" Sylvia said.

Shane caught a cab over to Caleb's apartment. He was sitting on the couch with a bottle of vodka in his hand when he arrived.

" What's going on Caleb?"

" *Fuck!* She blew me off man! She acted like she didn't even know me. I guess I deserve it." Caleb said as he turned the bottle up, gulping down as much vodka as he could stand at once.

" Hand me that bottle. Guess I'm staying here tonight. Let's get wasted!" Shane said deciding to stay with his friend for moral support. He knew Caleb would need it. He wasn't used to being rejected, or *being in love* with the woman that rejected him, for that matter. Shane knew he had his work cut out for him.

Mara was headed over to Caleb's apartment. They had planned to spend the weekend alone together, *for the first time*. He usually spent his weekends with the guys, but Sylvia wanted to be alone with Ryan, and Shane wanted to spend the weekend alone with Melissa in their apartment. That is when Caleb said he wanted her to spend the weekend with him. They have been a couple for several months now. Ryan had approached her friend Sylvia that night at the bar, *trying to pick her up*. He had explained the uncanny resemblance between her and the other Mara. It was still strange to her though, the fact they had the same name and looked alike, and ended up in the same place, and with the same man. *How often does that happen?* She had felt sorry for Caleb after hearing Ryan's account of the story. Thats when she had agreed to go out on a date with him. The rest is history, as they say. The other Mara has never reappeared, and she did not care if she ever did. Caleb was hers now. *It was her loss*. She'd never met anyone like Caleb, and she was deeply in love with him.

Caleb and Mara had a nice quiet dinner, and cuddled up on the couch to watch movies. Caleb still thought it odd that Mara did not remember that night they had spent together. He knew it was the same girl. The only difference was her eyes, they were a darker shad of blue, and not the grayish-blue he'd remembered. But, he could've easily mistaken that, he'd had quite a bit to drink that night. His shoulder had finally healed over, but, every time he had one of his nightmares it felt like someone set it on fire. His nightmares were coming less often now, he rarely had one anymore, and he was glad to be sleeping decent again. Caleb looked down at Mara, who was fast asleep, cradled in his arms.

" Mara, " Caleb whispered in her ear,"Wake up babe, let's go to bed."

Mara stirred, stretched, and opened her eyes.

" Sorry, I guess I am more tired than I thought. Bed sounds good."

They replaced the many cushions back on the couch, turned off the TV, and went to bed.

Mara kissed his lips, and climbed on top of him. She pulled her nightgown up over her head and threw it somewhere behind her. Caleb reached and fondled her breasts as he slid into her. He lifted up slightly to capture her lips, and ....

She began to change before his eyes. Horns appeared from each side of her head, the great bat-like wings spread out behind her, and her long-nailed hands became claws. She laughed, a deep throaty growl, and climbed off of him. As she walked around the bed, she began to change again. Her breasts sunk in and became the chest of a man. Her female figure began to grow wide, and more muscular. A large penis grew from between its legs. Caleb looked over to see Mara sleeping beside him. His shoulder hot, the scars were burning a bright fiery red. Caleb touched his shoulder , and quickly pulled his hand away. The smell of burning flesh assaulted his nostrils. He watched as the demon creature climbed atop Mara, and began moving within her. It groaned and growled, and smiled in Caleb's direction. Caleb reached to pull the creature from Mara,....it attacked. The creature lunged at him and wrapped its strong claws around his neck, squeezing the life out of him. Caleb swung at the beast, and it retaliated, and sunk its large fangs deep in the flesh of his burning shoulder..............*pain*.......

Caleb woke with a searing pain in his shoulder and jumped from his bed trying to catch his breath. He felt like he would suffocate.

" Caleb?" Mara woke as Caleb jumped from the bed.

" Yeah....." Caleb panting heavily trying to pull oxygen back into his lungs.

" Are you okay?" Mara said as she got out of bed and turned on the light.

" Oh, my god! Caleb, what happened?" Mara said, seeing the blood running from Caleb's shoulder, and the bruising around his neck.

" I had a nightmare, that's all." Caleb said finally able to breathe. He ran his hand through his hair, *damn.* His hand was severely burned.

" That was no nightmare Caleb. Nightmares don't leave marks." Mara said running over to him, and inspecting his wounds.

" Mara, ...where's your nightgown?" Caleb just seeing that she was stark naked.

Mara looked down at herself, her nightgown was gone, and there was blood smeared on the inside of her thighs dripping from small scratches that resembled claw marks. Caleb seeing them at the same time.

They exchanged looks that entailed both fear, and confusion.

Two months had passed since that frightful night. Caleb and Mara never spoke about it. There were no words that could describe, or explain, what they had experienced.. Caleb's nightmares seemed to stop completely after that night. Caleb was on his way back to their apartment, Mara said she had a surprise for him. She had recently moved in with him, and Caleb purposed to her only a few days ago. They had not set a date yet, but were thinking along the lines of a nice fall wedding. He found her sitting on the couch, holding something in her hand when he arrived.

" What's the big surprise? " Caleb asked, taking the small stick from her hand as she held it out to him.

Caleb looked down at it, then back up at her.

" Caleb, ...I'm pregnant.! We're going to have a baby!" Mara said, unable to hide her excitement.

 An overwhelming sense of fear washed over him as Caleb saw a flash of pale bluish- gray play across Mara's eyes, and his shoulder began to burn hotter than hell's fire.

The Dream ©2007

It was night. She could see the stars shinning bright against the black sky, and a full moon casted eerie shadows around her. *She was moving.* She could hear the loud roaring of an engine, and the sloshing of water. *A boat?* She couldn't be sure. Her head felt as if she'd been kicked by a mule, and stomach was churning, she felt sick. She tried to get up, but was too weak, and fell onto her back. *The engine stopped, only the sound of water.* A pair of hands drug her to her feet, and her legs threatened to buckle underneath her. She could see no arms, no shoulders, no face. *Only hands.* She felt as if she was being lifted, and then, falling. *A splash.* The water was cold, it stung her skin like a million tiny bee stings. She felt herself falling further, deeper. She tried to swim, reaching for the surface. But, her limbs failed her. She was numb, her muscles refusing to comply. She struggled against the black undertow, trying to kick her feet. *She couldn't*, something was tangled around her ankles. Her lungs burning as she sees the barely visible surface disappearing into the distance..........

Kendra woke up screaming. Her father rushed to her side, and wrapped his arms around her, trying to console her.

" It's okay Kendra, you were dreaming again." Blake said, gently rocking his daughter side to side. Kendra had been having nightmares for eight years. Her mother, Kelly, died tragically when Kendra was only nine. Kelly had been murdered. *Drowned.* She'd been suffering with these nightmares ever since. Blake had decided to put Kendra in therapy, although, it didn't help stop the nightmares, it did help Kendra deal with her issues concerning her mother's death.

" Are they ever going to stop, Daddy?" Kendra asked.

" I don't know, baby. I don't know." Blake said, letting her go now that she had calmed down.

" What do you say I take you out for breakfast before school. Come on, I'll drop you off on my way to work." Blake often took Kendra for breakfast at the local diner when she'd awaken from one of her nightmares. It had become almost routine for them. She did not have the dreams every night, but, they did come often, at least a few times a week. Blake hated the fact he could not take the nightmares from his little girl. Well, she wasn't so little anymore, she was seventeen. But, she was still daddy's little girl in his eyes.

" Okay, I'll be down in a few minutes." Kendra said, smiling at her father as he shut her bedroom door behind him.

" So what are you doing this weekend? I heard that Jake's parents are going to be out of town, and he's throwing a party tonight!" Shawn said. It was the last day of school, summer break, and Shawn wasn't gonna miss out on any chance to see Jake. *Her crush.* Shawnee, Shawn for short, has been Kendra's best friend since junior high. They were basically inseparable. They've always done everything together.

" Well, my dad's going up tonight to get the cabin ready. We are supposed to spend all next week up on the lake. But, I don't have to go with him. I can stay here. We're not going up until Monday. So that gives us a couple of days alone, if you want to stay at my house." Kendra explained, a little excited about the prospect of a party at Jake's. She knew that River would probably be there.

" Perfect! I'll tell my mom I'm staying over at your place, and then we'll head over to the party!"

" Okay, you can call her from my house."

" Kendra, call me if you need anything. I'll only be a day or two, then I'll be back to get you. Make sure your packed and ready. I love you. Bye Shawn." Blake said giving Kendra a peck on the forehead, waved to Shawn, and turned to get into his car.

Kendra and Shawn waved as he drove off. They watched until his tail lights were out of site. Then turned to go into the house.

"Let's get ready! Party starts in an hour!" Shawn squealed, as they locked the door behind them. Both girls ran upstairs to Kendra's room, intending on raiding the closet. They had to find something to wear.

Kendra parked the car across the street, and her and Shawn walked toward the party. Jake and River were on the front porch greeting their guests as they arrived.

" *Oh my god!* Look at all these people. I bet the whole high school is here. Shawnee, guess who I see!" Kendra said spotting Jake.

" Yep, and look who's standing beside him!" Shawn giggled.

" Well hello ladies!" River said taking Kendra's hand to help her up the stairs. Kendra looked beautiful, with her light green summer dress, and strapped heels that matched. Her long red hair setting off the color of her deep green eyes. " Can I get you a drink, Kendra?" River asked as he followed her into the house.

" Yeah, sure. What do you have?"

" Well, what do want?" River giving her a playful wink.

" Wine cooler?"

" Coming right up!" River said as he rushed over to the fridge, grabbed two coolers, and headed back to stand beside Kendra.

 " Here ya go. Hey...Kendra, you want to go somewhere a little less crowded?"

" Yeah, lets do. I can barely hear anything in here." The music was so loud she thought her head would explode if she had to hear much more of it. River grabbed her hand, and she turned to look for Shawn who had not followed her in. She spotted her outside standing with Jake, Shawn winked at her and waved her off, lipping that she'd catch up with her later. Kendra smiled, nodded her head, and followed River as he lead her through the sliding glass doors, and outside. He lead her down the wooden walkway toward the creek and past he shed.. Kendra stumbled as her heel got caught between two boards, and she almost fell. River grabbed her, holding her up as she straightened herself.

" Hold on. I'll get it." He said as he bent to free her shoe. "It's stuck pretty good.... there. I got it."

" Thanks." she said as he stood up to face her. River reached up and brushed a stray red hair from her eyes, as he leaned in and kissed her. Kendra smiled up at him as he slowly broke the kiss.

" Guess I'd better take these off, and carry them. " she said as she reached down and unstrapped her shoes. They walked hand-in-hand to the edge of the creek and sat down.

 " Wait, I'll be right back." River said as he got up and disappeared into the shed. He returned in seconds carrying a blanket, which he spread on the grass for them to sit on.

" I'd hate for you to ruin that pretty dress of yours. It looks good on you. " River flashing her a grin. He *was* handsome. He had sandy blond hair, and smiling blue eyes, with a boyish grin that lit up his whole face when he smiled.

" Yeah, thanks. I didn't even think about it. I'd hate to get grass stains on my green dress." Kendra said, and they both laughed.

" So what are your plans this summer?"

" I don't really have any. Me and my dad are going up to spend a week on the lake Monday. That's the only plans so far." Kendra said looking at the stars as she laid onto her back.

" Really. Where?" River asked.

" We have a cabin up on Cherokee lake."

" No way! So do we. I'll be there next week too! Maybe I'll see you there." River said not believing his luck, as he lay down beside her, and looked up at the night sky.

" Yeah. Maybe. I can meet you at the swimming area if you want."

" Sounds like a plan!" River said, as he leaned over and kissed her again. Kendra laid her head in the crook of his arm, her hand on his chest, and soon she was fast asleep.

River woke before Kendra and realized it was early morning. He must have fallen asleep shortly after she did. He only remembered watching her sleep in his arms. He had intended on waking her up after a few minutes.

" Kendra." he said nudging her gently in the shoulder. She stretched her arms and opened her eyes.

" Oh my god, did we....?"

" No, " River laughed, " we only fell asleep."

" Oh. What time is it?" She said as she reached for her shoes and slid her feet inside them." On second thought, I better carry them again."as she pulled them off again.

" It's 8 A.M.."

" Oh no! Shawn! I wonder if she found a ride home." Kendra just remembering her friend.

" I am sure Jake gave her ride. Don't worry." River said as he and Kendra folded the blanket, and walked over to the shed to put it away. They walked up the long wooden pathway and went inside the house.

" What a mess!" Kendra said, as she seen the havoc that a house full of drunken teenagers could reek.

" Yeah, I guess I'll stay awhile and help Jake clean up." River said noticing Jake and Shawn coming down the stairs.

Shawn smiled wide at Kendra, and gave her a wink. " I was wondering where you two ran off two." She said. Shawn had spent the night, too. The one place she'd wanted to for a long time. *Jake's bed.*

" I was wondering the same about you!" Kendra said returning her smile.

" I guess we are all that's left of the party. Everyone else is gone."Jake said.

" Want us to stay and help you guys clean up?" Kendra asked River.

" Sure, if you want. But, I am think me and Jake can handle it." he said.

" No, we'll stay and help!" Shawn said, not quite ready to leave Jake's side yet.

" I guess that settles it then, let's get started. Afterward, I'll take you all to lunch. Since it"s gonna be that time before we get done." Jake laughed, waving his hands at the mess that lay in every direction around them.

Kendra had invited River and Jake to hang out with them at her house tonight and watch movies. She knew her dad wouldn't be back until tomorrow afternoon, so she felt comfortable inviting them to stay over.

" So, you and Jake, huh?" Kendra asked smiling knowingly at her friend.

" Yeah, and *it was* great!" Shawn said.

" So, you two a couple now?"

" You know it! Isn't it exciting! What about you and River?"

" I don't know."

" Trust me girl, if you spent the night in his arms under the stars, you're a couple!" Shawn said.

" I guess we'll see right.....That's probably them now." Kendra said as the doorbell rang.

Shawn squealed, as her and Kendra went downstairs to let them in.

The hands. A pair of hands jerked her to her feet.

She felt herself being lifted, then falling.

A splash.

She was falling, further into the cold black depth. She struggled against it, to no avail. She felt the water rushing into her nose and mouth as she tried to scream, and claw her way to the surface. She tried to kick, but couldn't. Her feet were tangled in something? *Weeds*? No! This time she seen it! *Rope*...............

Kendra screamed, startling River from a light sleep.

" Kendra?! Are you all right?" River asked seemingly concerned.

" Yeah, I am okay. Just a nightmare." Kendra said noticing her and River had fallen asleep on the couch.

" Wow, that must have been some nightmare. You sounded like somebody was trying to kill you."

" Somebody was. " She said as River flashed her a puzzled look.

" Never mind, long story. I'll explain it some other time. Where's Jake and Shawn?"

" They went into the guest room a while ago. They're probably sleeping." River said.

" Yeah, I guess we need to get some sleep too." Kendra said as she got up from the couch and headed up the steps toward her room. Then stopped suddenly.

" You coming?"she yelled back at him, and River suddenly appeared beside her.

She laughed at how quickly he caught up.

" Might as well, since you invited me." He said, flashing her that handsome boyish grin of his.

Blake had readied the cabin, put the boat in the water, and stocked the cabin's food stores. Yep, everything was ready. He would pick up Kendra tomorrow. But, now, he was ready for a drink. He went into his office, and pulled a book off the shelf. He always had a bottle of whiskey stashed behind his legal books, he grabbed the bottle, and pushed the book back into its place. He sat down in his chair, and propped his feet up on the desk. He remembered how Kendra used to play in here while he was working on his cases. Her little doll house still sat in the far corner. Though now, it was gathering dust, it hadn't been played with in years, but, he couldn't bring himself to throw it out. *Man she was growing up.* She looked more like Kelly everyday. Blake turned the bottle up, and downed the last swallow. He went over to the bookshelves again, and grabbed another bottle. Taking a quick swig, and carrying it with him to the bedroom he and Kelly used to share during their many vacations at the cabin. He readied himself for bed, and slid under the cover. He reached over and sat his whiskey on the bedside table, and turned off the lamp.

Blake. The faint voice whispered. Blake stirred slightly, and rolled over.

Blake. She's mine, you can't have her. The voice spoke again.

This time, Blake heard it. He opened his eyes, and looked around.............

" Jesus!" he said, seeing the illuminated figure hovering just at the foot of his bed.

She's mine Blake. You can't have her. It spoke louder this time.

" What the hell do you want?! **Leave us alone**!" Blake shouted at her, hoping to scare the ghost away.

It approached him, and then flew over his head as Blake ducked to avoid it. Then back again past the bed side table, as his bottle of whiskey fell, shattering across the hardwood floor.

She was gone.

Blake turned on the bedside lamp, threw the cover over his head, and mumbled something incoherent, as he went back to sleep.

Kendra loved being at the cabin. It was a home away from home. It reminded her of her mother and all the time they'd spent together there. She was glad to get away for awhile, and excited at the opportunity to spend time with River again. She was supposed to meet him later this evening at the swimming area. They'd planned a night swim, alone together. But first, she had to finish unpacking.

" Dad, I am gone."

" Where are you going?"

" To meet some friends for a little night swimming. I won't be too late, I promise." Kendra said kissing Blake on the cheek, and headed out the door.

" Be careful! And have fun!" he yelled out the door to her, as she walked towards the swimming area. She waved at him and smiled, then continued on the path. Blake went into his office, pulled out a bottle of whiskey, and settled himself at his desk.

" Hi." She said as she walked over to River, who was looking out over the lake.

" Hi." he said as he turned to face her.

River greeted Kendra with a light kiss, and helped her to spread out the blanket she'd brought along.

" You ready for a swim?" he asked her. Kendra nodded her head as she slipped off her shorts, and kicked her sandals to the side.

" I'll race you!" Kendra said as she broke into a run toward the water, laughing. River close on her heels.

He was watching her. Well hidden in the trees, he sat watching as she slipped further away from him. She seemed so carefree frolicking in the water with her young lover. How dare she do this right under his nose. *Did she think he didn't know? That he wouldn't find out?* He watched as the young man carried her from the water and lay her onto the blanket. Watched as he kissed her lips, and ran his fingers through her red hair. He watched as he made love to her, right out in the open. *She didn't even have the decency to hide it!* A deep rage was building within him, threatening to overtake his reality. *Cheating Bitch!*

River walked Kendra backed to her cabin, and kissed her goodnight. They made plans to go water skiing tomorrow after lunch, and she couldn't wait. Kendra waved at him as he turned, and headed for his own cabin. She turned to go inside, her body still reeling, from the memories of his touch, knowing she was in love with him.

" Dad, I'm back!" Kendra yelled. No answer. Kendra went to his bedroom. Maybe he was already sleeping. She opened the door carefully, so she would not wake him. He wasn't there.

" Dad?" Kendra called to him again. Again, no answer. *The office,* she thought. He was probably having his nightcap. She opened the door, and peered inside. The lights were off, and he wasn't there. She started to close the door when something caught her eye. A figure quickly ran past the door. Kendra turned on the light. No one. She went inside the office to look around, but didn't find anything. Again she turned to leave the office, as a piece of paper flew from one of the bookshelves, and drifted, landing just at her feet. Kendra bent to pick it up, opening the folded paper.

" What the...?" Kendra was in shock at what she saw. It was a portion of divorce papers. There was a request for sole custody, in exchange for no alimony payments. The house, and all property was to be sold and profits equally split. Kendra's eyes grew wide as she read her own name, and the names of her parents.

" *Oh my god.*" she whispered.

The paper slipping from her fingers to the floor, as arms wrapped tight around her, and a pair of hands pressed a damp white cloth over her nose and mouth. Kendra struggled against the tight grip, but it was no use. Her limbs were becoming numb, and she felt as if she was going to pass out. The world started spinning around her, then........ there was nothing.

Kendra opened her eyes to see the stars glittering bright against the black sky. Although, they seem to blur in and out, as she tried to focus on them. *She was moving.* She could hear the load roaring of an engine, and the faint sloshing sound of water. *Was she on a boat?* She wasn't sure. Her head was still swimming, and her stomach felt as if she would be sick. The sound of the engine suddenly disappeared. The sound of water was slightly louder than before. Then.... she heard something else......someone talking.

" You can't have her, damn it. I won't let you take her from me!" Blake yelled at the ghostly figure hovering before him.

She's mine Blake. Kelly said. *She's mine.*

" NO!!" he yelled again, throwing his empty whiskey bottle against the side of the boat, shattering it into tiny glittering pieces, as Kelly's ghost disappeared to the back of the boat.

A pair of hands reached for her, pulling Kendra to her feet. Her knees buckled under her, and she felt herself being lifted. Something was pulling at her ankles. *Oh god.* Was she dreaming again?

" You're not taking my little girl, Kelly. You're not taking *anything* from me." Blake said as he lifted her high onto his shoulders.

" Daddy?" Kendra whispered, recognizing his voice.

" Shut up, Kelly!"

" Daddy its me Kendra." she said, her voice weak and shaky.

Fear struck Kendra hard as she felt herself falling.... she knew what was next, she braced herself for the cold water below...........................

as she landed hard onto the floor of the boat knocking the wind out of her.

She heard a struggle, then a splash. Then someone was touching her ankles.

" Kendra, be still. " River said as he untied the rope around her ankles, and helping her sit upright.

" Are you okay?" he asked, concerned about her condition.

 Kendra looked up at him, as he wrapped his arms around her.

" River..." Kendra said her eyes streamed with tears as she seen her father's lifeless body floating face down in the dark water.

They sat holding one another, as they watched a ghostly apparition slowly fade where it had been hovering just above his body.

www.ingramcontent.com/pod-product-compliance
Lightning Source LLC
Chambersburg PA
CBHW020647130626
46552CB00003B/1440